Stanley Bags

AND THE RATHER DANGEROUS M

By
Bob Wilson

PUFFIN BOOKS

In Huddersgate - [famed for its tramlines]
up north where it's boring and slow,

Stanley Bagshaw resides with his Grandma
at number 4 Prince Albert Row.

He was down by Cope's pond, spotting tadpoles
and had spotted one hundred and four,

When he noticed this hole in the mudbank
what he'd never noticed before.

So he took off his shoes and his stockings and paddled across nice and slow,

and was just bending down to inspect it,

when......

a water-rat bit his big toe.

It turned septic, and old Doctor Flynn sent him up to the hospital clinic, and the doctors up there kept him in.

When Grandma had finished her story, she just carried on with her meal, But Stanley sat there, very quiet.

He was thinking how Edward must feel.

Old Edward was feeling much better,
but he lay on his bed in the ward,
and stared up at a crack in the ceiling.
He didn't feel ill now – just bored.

Gloom, fed-upness, lethargy, torpor...
boredom...langour   gloom.

The rest of the patients were bored too.
So a kind nurse thought she would try
to cheer them all up a little
by starting a game of 'I-Spy'.

You seem to be really
interested in that book.
What's it about?

Accountancy.

I spy with my little eye...
Something beginning with T

Old Edward stared out of the window, down to the gardens below.

He wished he was out there with nature, and at visiting times he felt low.

I've brought you some flowers, [said Stanley].

They look really beautiful.

Mint ba[...]

Ooh thanks Ted

Edward put Stanley's flowers in a beaker,
and gave the young lad a boiled sweet,
and told him some stories about nature,
and said he'd been cheered up a treat.

I hope you're not feeling too bad.

Flowers, for me!?
[said Edward]
Eeeh Stan you're a good little lad.

This is a very rare plant called... 'a weed'

This man is a genius.

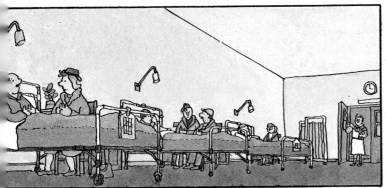

But visiting time was soon over,
A nurse came in, banging a gong,

and announced in a voice like a fog-horn –

Time's up everyone.
Come along!

The visitors said goodbye quickly,
seemed anxious to get to the door.

But Stanley gave Edward a cuddle.

And then gave him two or three more.

By the time Stan was out in the corridor,

the rest of the people had gone.

Our Stanley just nodded his head.

But the signs were all rather confusing
The big words looked all foreign to Stan.

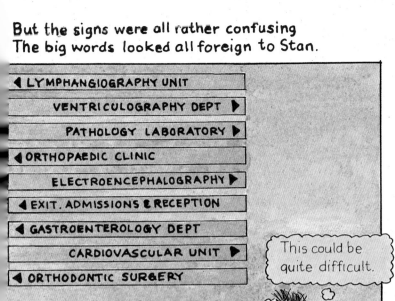

◄ LYMPHANGIOGRAPHY UNIT
VENTRICULOGRAPHY DEPT ►
PATHOLOGY LABORATORY ►
◄ ORTHOPAEDIC CLINIC
ELECTROENCEPHALOGRAPHY ►
◄ EXIT. ADMISSIONS & RECEPTION
◄ GASTROENTEROLOGY DEPT
CARDIOVASCULAR UNIT ►
◄ ORTHODONTIC SURGERY

This could be quite difficult.

He decided he'd just have a wander about.

Eeeny..meeny..

..miney......

..Mo!

And that's how the danger began!

For the corridors went on for ever it seemed and each one was the same as the next.

Not one seemed to lead to the way out, and our Stan became rather perplexed.

I could be trapped in here for ever!

1

You look happy.

I go home soon

2

Then...

He came to a door marked...

THEATRE
Surgical
Ward
number
3

I didn't know nurses did acting!
[thought Stan].

So he opened the door just to see.

Inside there was lots of equipment,
and a couch with all lights overhead.

I am feeling tired,
[thought Stanley]
I've been wandering about for so long.

This must be the visitors' rest-room,
[thought Stan].

But that's where our Stanley thought wrong!

It didn't look much like a theatre stage.
It looked more like a sun-bathing bed.

Sir George Oswald Nash the eye-surgeon, and Doctor Emanuel Mason,

were in the next room getting ready, for a dangerous eye operation.

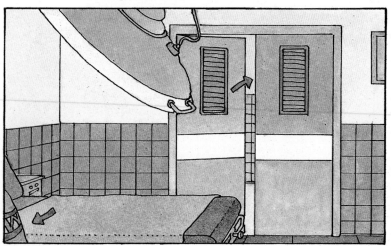

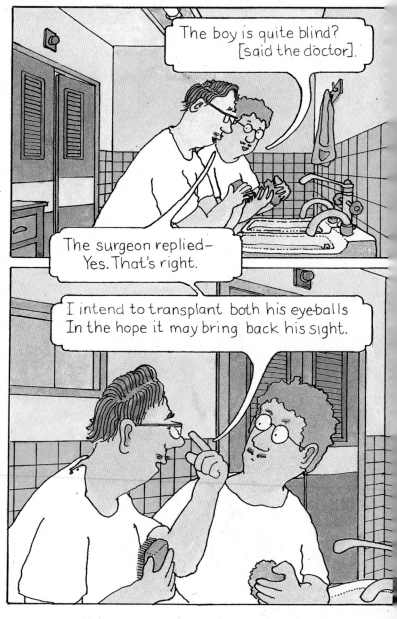

And there on the table, lay Stanley
So pale...and so still...and so small.

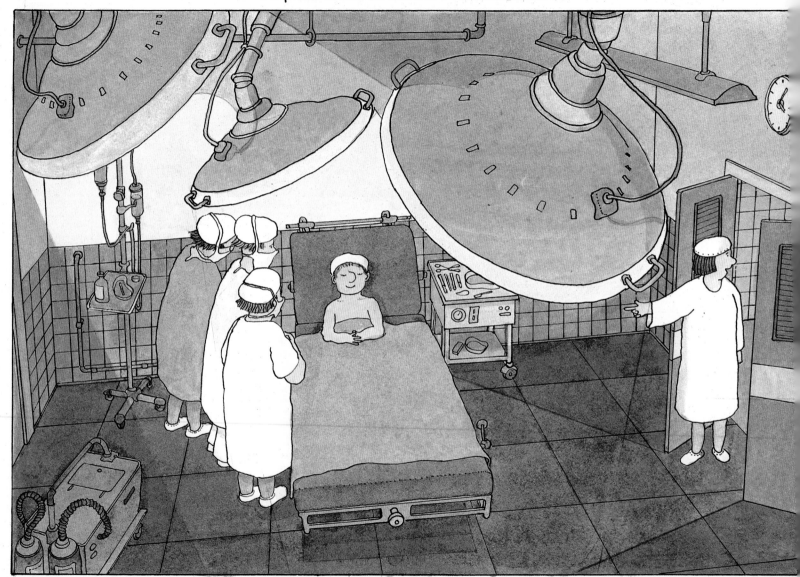

The doctors and nurses were all rather tense,

Our Stanley was happily dreaming,
with the hospital lights beaming down.
He was dreaming he was in a desert,
on a sun-bathing bed getting brown.

But our Stan wasn't worried at all.

A figure came slowly towards him in a long flowing gown and a mask.

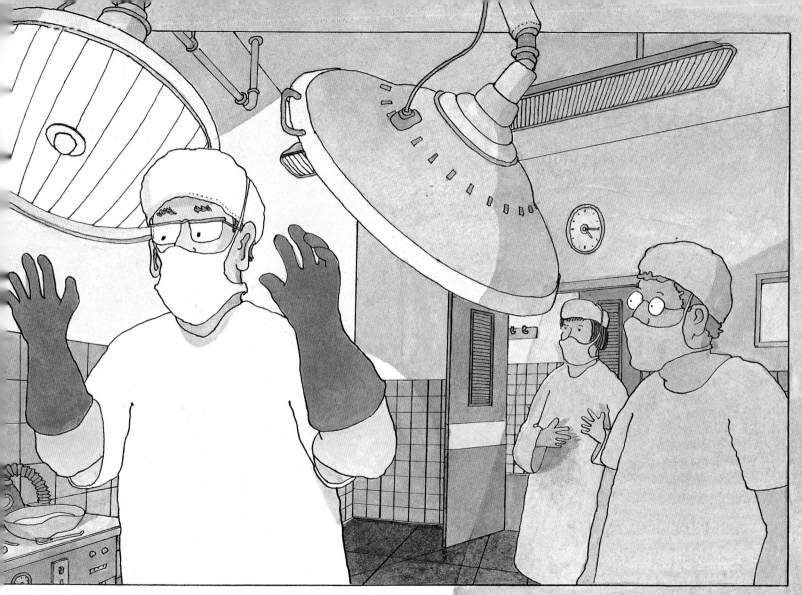

The surgeon advanced to the table. He was feeling quite tense, about to commence
In his eyes there was deep concentration a most difficult eye operation.

But first he addressed his assistants,

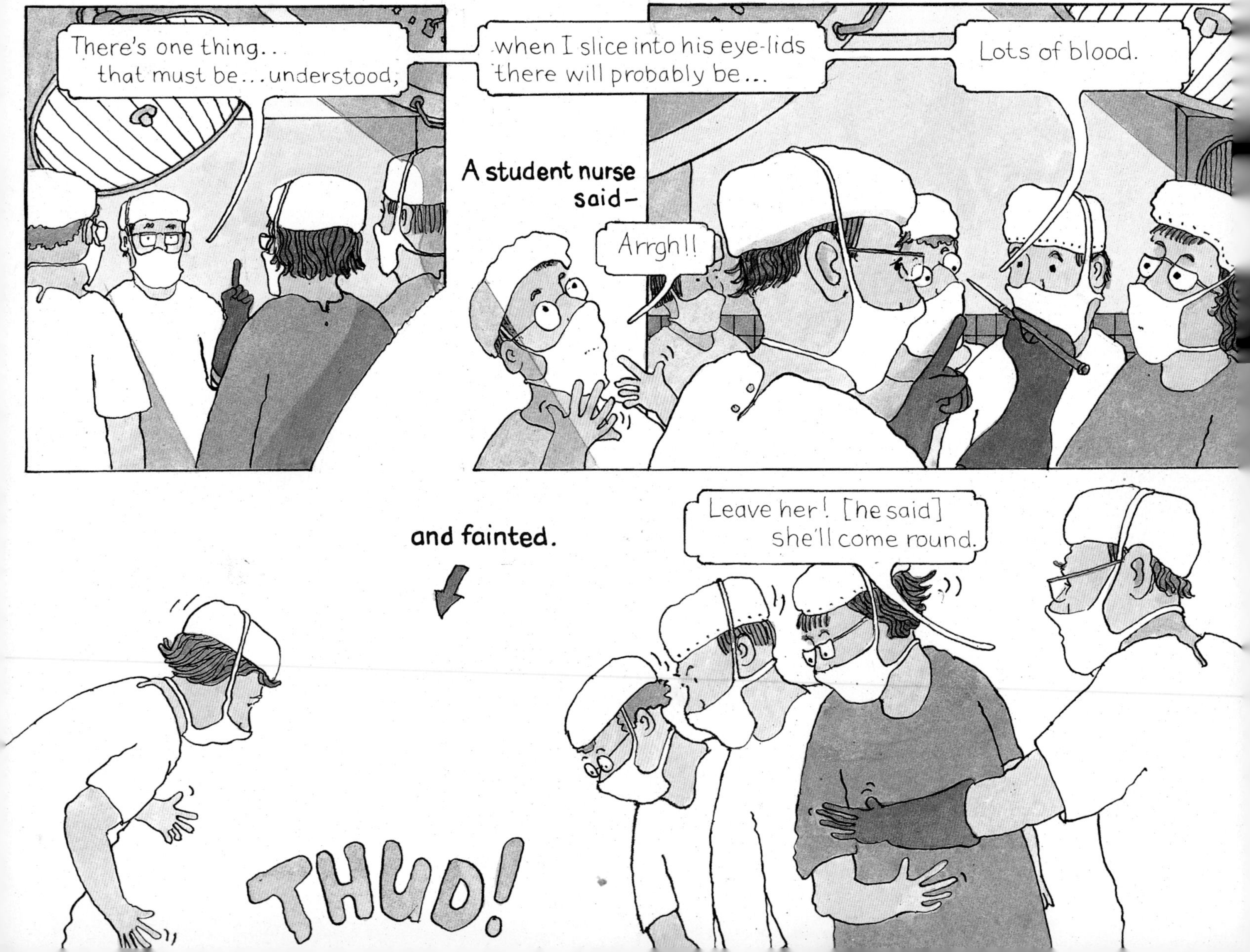

Then, placing one hand on Stan's forehead,

I will now make the primary incision, and I want there to be not a sound.

with the skill of a surgeon supreme,
he got ready to cut...and would have done............. __But__

. . . . At that point Stan woke from his dream.

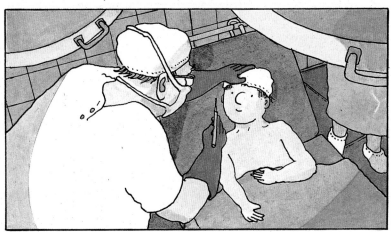

And seeing the surgeon above him,
in his long flowing gown and his mask,
said –

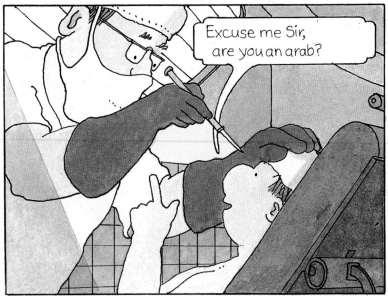

Excuse me Sir,
are you an arab?

The surgeon said –
No, why do you ask?

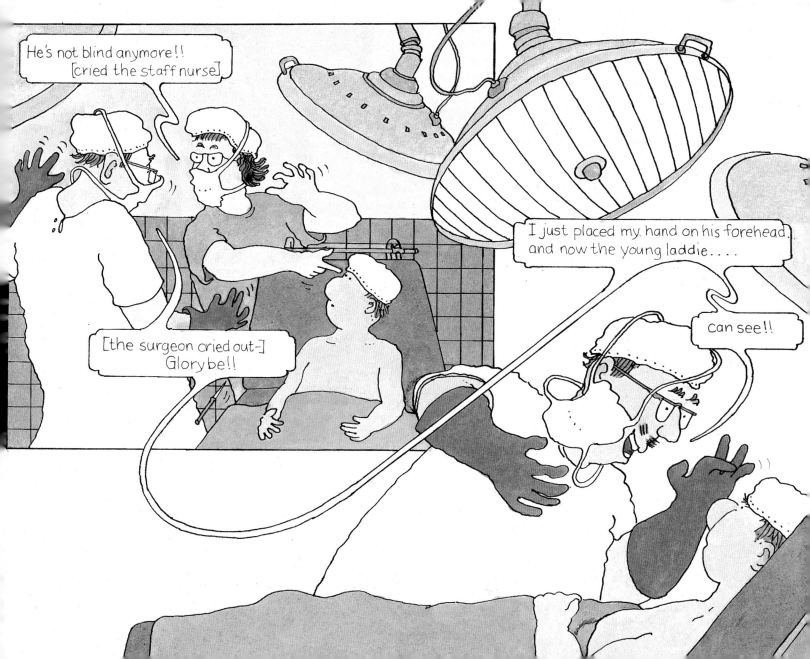

And..

Oh, to be sure, it's a miracle cure!

which seemed, to our Stan, rather odd.

How do you feel!? [said the surgeon], Now that, at last, you can see?

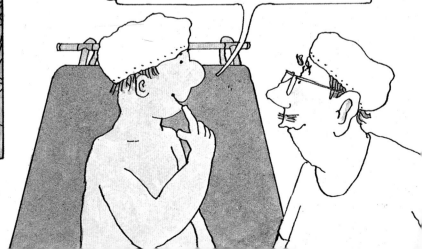

I feel a bit hungry, [said Stanley]. I'd better get home for my tea.

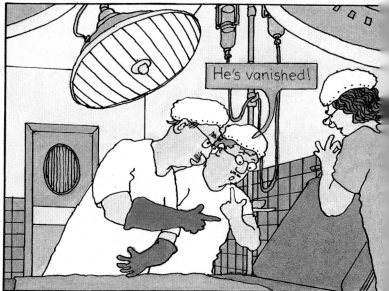

NOT QUITE THE END